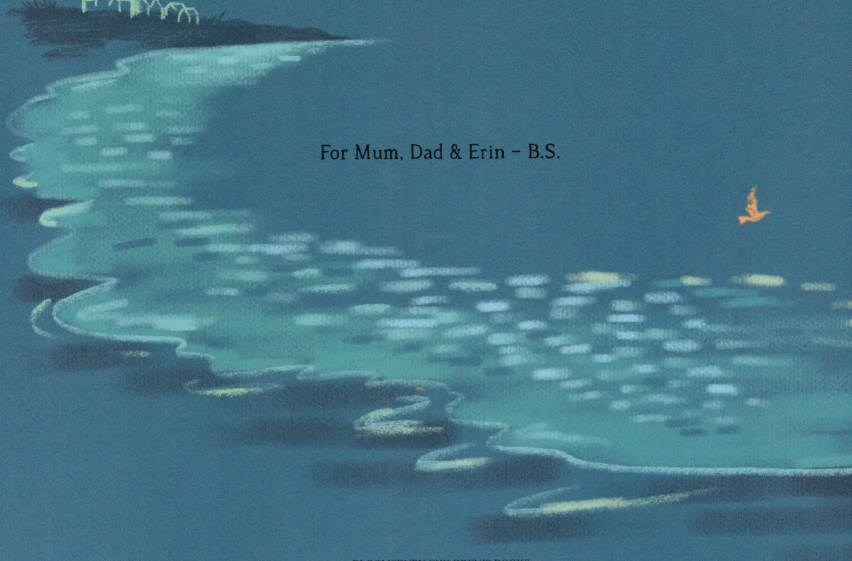

For Mum, Dad & Erin – B.S.

BLOOMSBURY CHILDREN'S BOOKS
Bloomsbury Publishing Plc
50 Bedford Square, London WC1B 3DP, UK
Bloomsbury Publishing Ireland Limited
29 Earlsfort Terrace, Dublin 2, D02 AY28, Ireland

BLOOMSBURY, BLOOMSBURY CHILDREN'S BOOKS and the Diana logo are trademarks of Bloomsbury Publishing Plc

First published in Great Britain by Bloomsbury Publishing Plc, 2025

Text copyright © Jordan Stephens, 2025
Illustrations copyright © Beth Suzanna Harris, 2025

Jordan Stephens and Beth Suzanna have asserted their rights under the Copyright, Designs and Patents Act, 1988,
to be identified as the Author and Illustrator of this work

All rights reserved. No part of this publication may be: i) reproduced or transmitted in any form, electronic or mechanical, including photocopying, recording or by means of any information storage or retrieval system without prior permission in writing from the publishers; or ii) used or reproduced in any way for the training, development or operation of artificial intelligence (AI) technologies, including generative AI technologies. The rights holders expressly reserve this publication from the text and data mining exception as per Article 4(3) of the Digital Single Market Directive (EU) 2019/790

A catalogue record for this book is available from the British Library

ISBN 978 1 5266 1806 1 (HB)
ISBN 978 1 5266 1807 8 (PB)
ISBN 978 1 5266 1808 5 (eBook)

1 3 5 7 9 10 8 6 4 2

Printed and bound in China by Leo Paper Products, Heshan, Guangdong

To find out more about our authors and books visit www.bloomsbury.com and sign up for our newsletters
For product safety related questions contact productsafety@bloomsbury.com

See for YOURSELF

Written by
Jordan STEPHENS

Illustrated by
Beth SUZANNA

BLOOMSBURY
CHILDREN'S BOOKS
LONDON OXFORD NEW YORK NEW DELHI SYDNEY

Harry Arco's family was obsessed with the sky. His dad, his dad's dad, and his dad before him, had ALL been pilots.

When they were flying up high,
surfing the wind with the birds,
they could see everything...

CLOUDS!

EAGLES!

STARS!

They felt on top of the world.

But Harry was different.

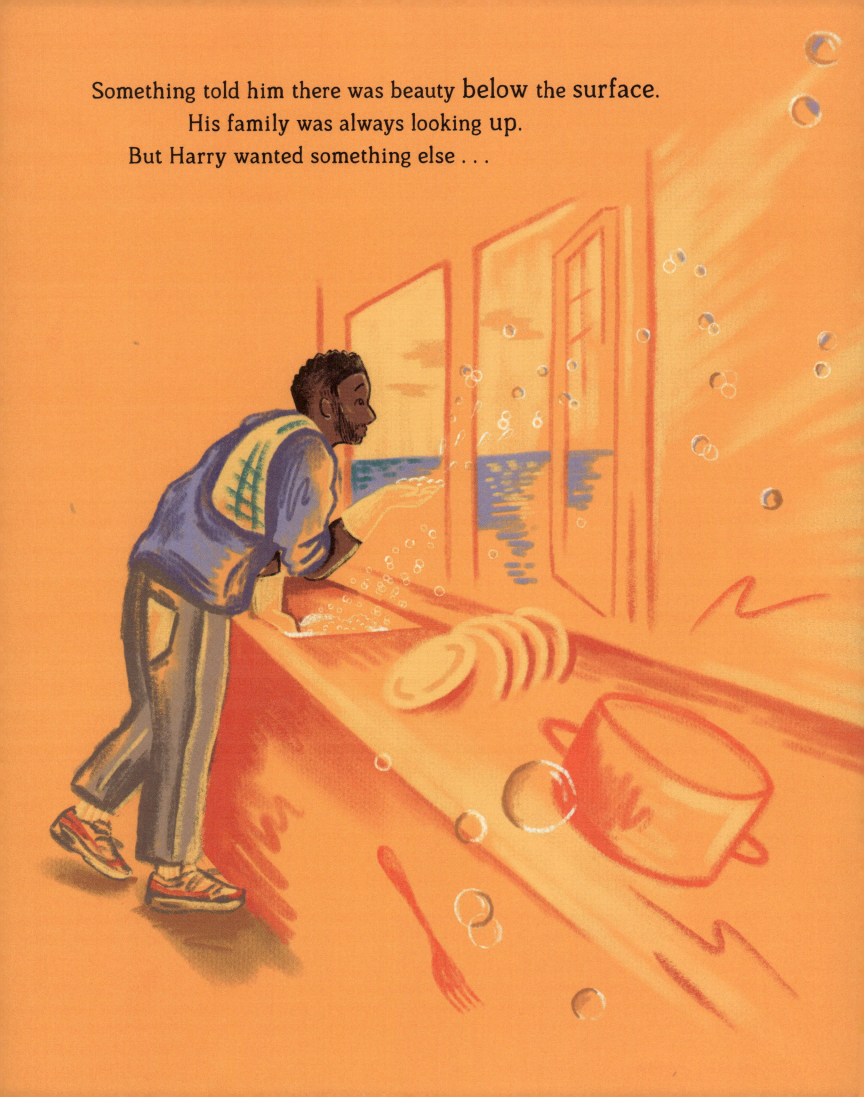

Something told him there was beauty below the surface.
His family was always looking up.
But Harry wanted something else . . .

Harry wanted to look down.

"Dad," he said. "Where's the bottom of the world?"

His dad laughed. "That's a funny question, Harry! At the bottom of the sea, I suppose."

"Has anyone ever seen it?"

"I don't think so.
           It's very, very deep."

"I want to go!" said Harry.
"Will you help me?"

His dad paused for a moment. Then he decided that **trust** in his son was more **important** than **fear** of the **unknown**.

"All right. Let's help you **see** it for **yourself**."

THEY WERE READY!

"No Arco has **ever** done this before," said Harry's dad. "But I **believe** in you. You can do it."

"I'll be back soon!" said Harry. "Promise!"

"Good luck!" his dad called.
And with a big breath
he sent him on his way.

Harry was instantly surrounded by
shimmering, glimmering fish.
They swam all around him, tiny sparks of colour
dancing like leaves in the breeze.

Harry grinned as he followed them down.

The further he went,
the bigger the fish became.
He plunged past
sharks and turtles.

He passed mighty whales whose shadows cast dark shapes all around him.

Then the sea began to lose light altogether, and the creatures grew odder and odder.

Squid,

octopus,

jellyfish.

Animals with no bones that looked like runny eggs.

Soon there was no light at all.
The blue got blacker and the water became night.

Harry was a long, long way
from the surface.

He was far, far away from his dad.

But he believed in his dream so he carried on down, down, down, until . . .

UD!

He was in **TOTAL DARKNESS**.

"This is it!" thought Harry. "I've made it. I've gone deeper than any Arco ever before."

He was surrounded by – **NOTHING**.

He waited. And then, suddenly, out of the shadows . . .

A huge wave of joy rushed over him.
He could SEE EVERYTHING!

Every worry became
a dancing shape . . .

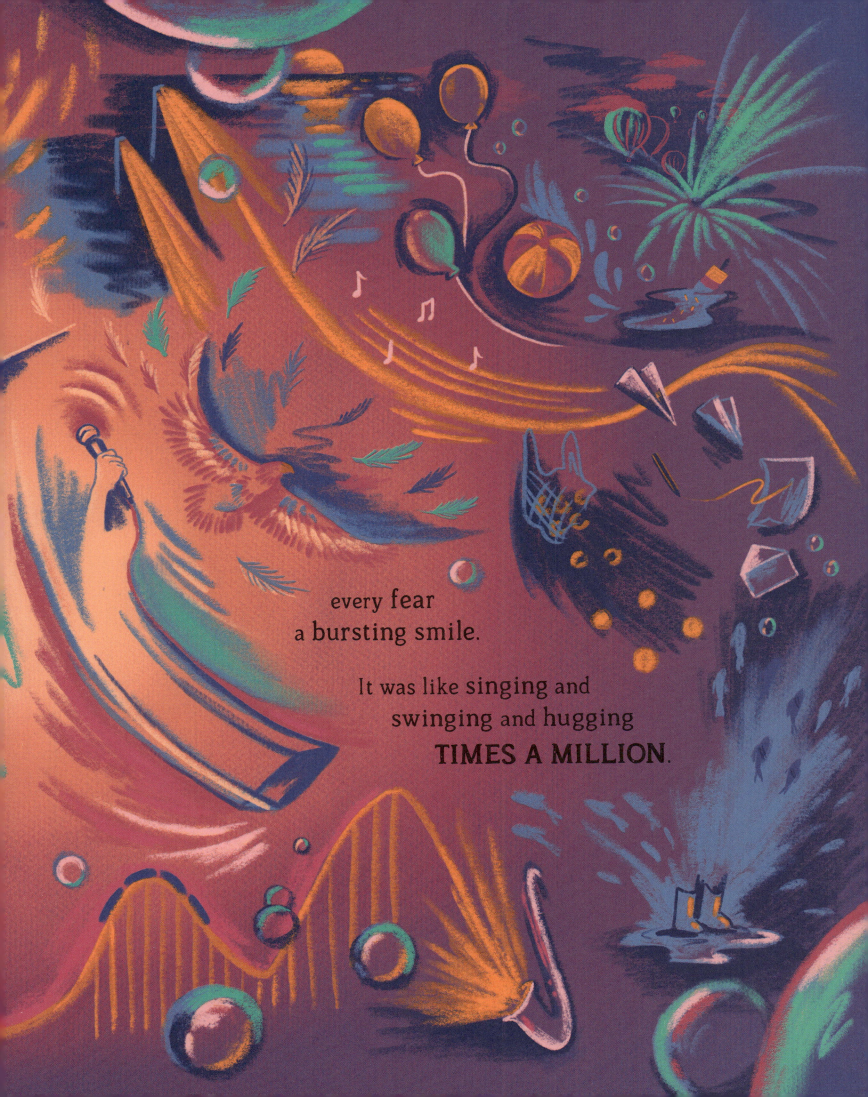

every fear
a bursting smile.

It was like singing and
swinging and hugging
TIMES A MILLION.

Harry had been right. There *is* so much beauty **beneath** the surface, so much to **see**, to **feel** and to **know**.

He couldn't wait to tell his dad.
He pressed his up-button and . . .

WHOOSH!

He shot back up!

"Dad!" he cried. "I made it! I went to the deepest place there is!"

His dad rushed to hug him hello.
"You did it! How do you feel?"

Harry's smile was a warm ray of sunshine.
"I feel like I'm on the BOTTOM of the world!" he said, laughing.

Later, Harry asked his dad, "How long was I gone?"

"No time at all," his dad replied.

"That's weird. It felt like forever."

"I'm so proud of you," said his dad. "What was it like down there?"

Harry smiled . . .